THE CHILLING CROSSBOW KILLER

By Brian Radford

Published by New Generation Publishing in 2019

First Edition

www.newgeneration-publishing.com

This book is dedicated to my special five-year-old grandson, Noah, who has begun his writing - and reading - career as a bright student at a South Wales primary school.

JUNE 3, 2018…3.00pm

`ABER Tidy's booming town clock struck three on this steaming hot Sunday afternoon.

Doolally Valley police had been called to Bluebell Woods where a dog walker had literally stepped on a body hidden under bracken and broken branches.

Supt. Peter Matthews was first on the scene, along with police cadets, Eddie Lewis and Edwyn Smith, both 22, who now represented the full Force, plus sergeant Ron Griffiths, after hefty Government cuts had removed three experienced officers.

Wide strips of blue-and-white police tape cordoned off the crime scene where Supt. Matthews and his young team slowly tip-toed towards the body.

Supt. Matthews pulled on a pair of well-worn plastic gloves, and carefully took away the bracken to reveal a man's body, flat out on its back, brutally murdered by an arrow fired into his heart.

It was bank manager Bertie Brown, popular to those who borrowed money, but not so popular to those he turned down.

"Definitely not suicide!" chuckled Matthews, attempting to bring a smile to the drained faces of Lewis and Smith, which were as pale as the one staring up at them.

Matthews politely declined help from Scotland Yard, confident that Aber Tidy was such a small community that catching the killer would be a simple formality. Well, he was in for a seismic shock…

Like so many other Welsh towns, Aber Tidy had its fair share of violence, robberies, drugs, and drunks, but never a murder.

News of the killing swept through the streets like a tidal wave. Terrified families double-locked their doors, closed the curtains, and communicated only by telephone.

Rev. Stuart Atkinson, popular new minister at St.

Mary's Anglican church, promptly cancelled Evensong, and every pub called 'time' before the clock struck nine, except for The Bell, where a team of forensic experts had just checked in.

Pathologist, Dr. Philip Barnett, was sure the murder was committed 24 hours earlier, which placed it right in the middle of the annual 'Festival on the Green'.

Around 100 people were enjoying the jugglers, Punch and Judy, a dog show, two towering clowns on stilts, and browsing in 20 tents that offered a wide range of affordable items from jewellery to cat blankets.

And for those attracted to quality music, the highly acclaimed Doolally Valley Orchestra was playing Mozart and Beethoven on the bright green bandstand that still smelled of fresh paint.

The tombola tent was closest to Bluebell Woods, but international kayak champions, Pete and Di, who ran it, saw and heard nothing suspicious.

Truth is, Pete and Di were also Wales' chatterbox champions, and wouldn't have noticed if a satellite had landed on their canvas top.

Sergeant Griffiths was relaxing with his fishing rod at Aber Tidy lake, amusing the Doolally Angling Club with his priceless one-liners, when Supt. Matthews rang his mobile.

Suddenly, the blissful Sunday silence was blown apart by the formidable Llanelli Male Voice choir exploding into life with 'Bread of Heaven', the Principality's rousing rugby anthem, worth ten points even before the game began.

High-speed Griffiths was at the crime scene inside 30 minutes, soaking up all that Supt. Matthews was able to tell him at this early stage.

There were no fresh tyre marks in the narrow, dusty lane that led to the woods, which made it simple for Matthews to establish that the assassin had not driven there to commit the crime.

"In which case," he spluttered, "how in heaven's name

did the killer carry the crossbow through that crowd without it being seen?"

Sgt Griffiths guessed, "Well, maybe he was already in the woods waiting for Brown, sir."

"Doubt it," countered Supt. Matthews. "It's more likely that Bertie was waiting there by arrangement, and the killer fired the arrow from 20 to 30 yards, while he stood at the edge of the Green."

A forensic officer, clad from head to toe in a pristine white protective plastic suit, carefully withdrew the deadly arrow, which revealed a shiny steel point.

Bertie had dressed appropriately for the Festival in a bright yellow-and-green sweater, lime green slacks, and a brand new pair of shiny black shoes. The sweater was now bright red from the bloody attack.

Women's police officer, WPC Hannah Thomas, a recent recruit from West Wales, accompanied Sgt Griffiths to break the appalling news to Bertie's wife, Wendy, and teenage sons, Stephan and Francis.

They lived in a delightful four-bed, detached cottage, alongside the cricket ground in Meadow Lane, which Bertie had aptly named Cover Drive.

Bluebell Woods was now teeming with media people pouring in from London, and all striving to get close to the body, but being firmly held back by Lewis and Smith, while the forensic squad erected a white tent to conceal the grim scene.

Five officers from around the Valley were being speedily drafted in after Supt. Matthews finally conceded that he required urgent support.

Pathologist, Phil Barnett, excitedly beckoned Matthews to the busy tent after noticing a white sheet of paper that had been forced into Brown's left hand.

Between them, they carefully eased it out, opened it up, and saw a chilling message printed in red capital letters.

Supt. Matthews whispered it to himself, "One done, two to go." And it was spookily signed OLIVA.

Even 20 years of police work, often shocking and

gruesome, hadn't prepared him for anything like this, and his body went ice cold.

Then he ordered Lewis and Smith to dig into Bertie Brown's background, smartly adding that two Eds were better than one.

Desperate for even a tiny clue, he demanded: "Focus on everyone who's been refused a loan or was being forced to pay one back."

Sgt Griffiths returned alone to the station, leaving WPC Thomas to comfort Wendy Brown, who was adamant that her husband of 20 years didn't have a single enemy.

" So, what didn't she know about Bertie that had led to his savage murder?" pondered Griffiths.

"That's our job to find out, and to find out fast!" snapped Supt. Matthews.

"Somewhere in this town, a next-door neighbour or, maybe a shop worker who wishes you a good day, is a ruthless killer, who has threatened to strike again.

"And why a crossbow? And who has the steady-hand and eagle eye to hit a target from a distance? There's no time to waste. We'll start fresh in the morning."

MONDAY, JUNE 4, 2018.

The Gazette's biggest headline in its 76 years, greeted early-morning readers with CHILLING CROSSBOW KILLING!

Supt. Matthews said he had never encountered such a difficult task since taking two months to complete a 2,000-piece jigsaw that, ironically, pictured a Welsh forest.

Chairs and tables were assembled in the town hall for Supt. Matthews to address the media.

He said, grimly: "Mr. Bertie Brown, a very popular bank manager, has been killed by an arrow fired with pinpoint accuracy from a crossbow in Bluebell Woods.

"And we have good reason to fear that the killer may strike again.

"In all probability this person lives and works in Doolally Valley, so we advocate great care and vigilance.

"We would appreciate any information that could help to find this person which, as always, would be treated in absolute confidence. That's all for now. Thank you."

Aber Tidy, which enjoyed a lively community spirit, was gripped by shock and fear. Bedroom lights had remained switched on throughout the night across the town.

Butcher Tom Thomas had even placed a sharpened meat cleaver under his pillow, but was still too scared to close his eyes.

By early afternoon, Morgan Jenkins, millionaire owner of Jenkins Properties, had put up a £20,000 reward for information leading to the arrest and conviction of Bertie Brown's killer.

Supt. Matthews was in overdrive. He had urgently requested a quick delivery of all film footage of the town's five CCTV cameras for the whole of Saturday.

Town Council administration boss, Joe Grierson, rushed them to Matthews in two large cardboard boxes.

Joe, a gifted joker, enjoyed recalling the day he was

almost thrown off a cruise liner in Barcelona when, dressed smartly in a cream jacket and black tie, he convinced the bar staff that he was the new captain, and he walked off with three packets of crisps, four Mars bars, and two tins of Tango.

"A pleasure to serve you, sir," gushed the flattered Nepalese barman. "Have it on us!"

Joe's angry wife Mo, popularly known as 'No' (No Mo!) forced him to return what was left, as he had already eaten the crisps, and drunk a tin of Tango.

Thankfully, Captain Adrian Adams, saw the funny side of it and allowed Joe and Mo (Moyra) to stay on board.

Two experienced police officers were soon crouched in front of a screen that was showing footage of the crowded Green in mid-afternoon on Saturday.

It was timed at 3.13pm, and the 20-strong orchestra was closing its first half with a medley of popular Welsh hymn tunes – Calon Lan, Cwm Rhondda, Blaenwern, and the lesser known Hengoed – before drifting off to the ice-cream van.

Bertie Brown could be seen strolling alone at the North end of the Green, close to the back lane that leads into the town, and approximately 100 yards from Bluebell Woods.

He stopped for a few seconds, and casually waved to someone on the opposite side of the road, who was standing in the black shadow of a long, towering hedge, and could not be identified.

Bertie then ambled over to him, and they chatted for less than a minute before disappearing into the shadow.

Supt. Matthews accepted that this was probably the last recorded sighting of Bertie Brown, but there was no useful clue of the person he met, except that it was a male of around 5ft 10in., which accounted for at least 100 of the same height in Doolally Valley alone.

The CCTV footage then switched to the bandstand area where the musicians were slowly returning to begin the second half.

Meanwhile, a fractious Supt. Matthews was adamant

that the arrow was so well honed that a professional carpenter had to be involved, and presumed that the crossbow was of the same high quality.

With this in mind, he summoned two officers to trawl through all available information about carpenters who traded in the Valley.

They found three—Glyn Morgan, John Swales and, rather appropriately, Dan Wood.

Moving swiftly, the officers contacted Bertie's deputy, Allan Mercado, asking for immediate access to classified information at the bank.

Above all else, the police were desperate to know whether any of these three carpenters was a client there.

Allan Mercado cooperated brilliantly. He disclosed that Dan Wood had been a client for more than ten years up to two weeks ago when he went off in a huff to Barclays after Bertie had refused to lend him £50,000.

Supt. Matthews practically purred, and raised both hands with fingers crossed.

"Let's go!" he called to Sgt. Griffiths, and they headed off at high speed to Dan Wood's home in Grange Road, less than 100 yards from Bluebell Woods.

Sgt. Griffiths pressed the doorbell hard to stress that it was urgent, and not Avon calling!

An elderly lady, peering through thick spectacles, pulled back the security latch, and peeped through a gap in the partly opened door.

Sgt. Griffiths got straight to the point… "Good afternoon, sorry to trouble you, but we are police officers wanting to speak to Mr. Dan Wood. I'm Sergeant Ron Griffiths, and this is Superintendent Peter Matthews."

Both officers produced identity cards, and the lady shakily responded, "I'm Dan's mother, and I'm looking after the cottage while he, Phyllis, and the children are on holiday. They're in Lanzarote, and will be back tomorrow."

Supt. Matthews felt all the air gush from his body. He was deflated and speechless. His prime suspect had been eliminated before he'd even met him.

Sgt Griffiths was typically blunt… "Well, that's one we can cross off," he said, shaking his head in deep disappointment.

"I'm not so sure!" snapped Supt. Matthews. "We could have a smart guy here. I'm not ruling him out just yet."

And he recalled a fascinating murder case when learning police skills as a young constable in the Met in London.

He said: "A young teacher was killed in Brixton, and everything pointed to his next-door neighbour. They'd had a big fall-out over a wooden panel in a fence that separated their gardens.

"But when we called on the neighbour, we were told he was on holiday in Marbella, and wouldn't be back for a week.

"But my inspector, Geoff Bayliss, wasn't satisfied with what we were told, and insisted on setting up a covert investigation into the neighbour.

"Geoff was convinced that the holiday was a charade, and that a hit-man had been paid to do the dirty work, and it turned out that he was absolutely right.

"Now, could Dan Wood have done the same? How convenient for him to be away at this critical time."

Matthews was at his cynical best. When he got a bee in his bonnet, it buzzed for days,

Close scrutiny of the town's CCTV footage continued…

"Come and look at this guv," an officer called to Matthews.

He was still perusing film taken from a camera high up on a post at the edge of the Green, and he was sure that the man walking away from all the fun and games was Bertie Brown. His unique stoop made it impossible for it to be anyone else.

It was another camera, and a different angle, to back up the earlier footage that showed Bertie crossing the road to meet the stranger, and then vanishing together in the shadow.

Supt. Matthews instantly conceded, "Well, that rules out a hit-man. Bertie clearly knew the guy he walked off with. It was all arranged. Nothing accidental about that! Nothing random.

"And he can't have had the crossbow with him in the street, so he must have hidden it in the woods, and killed Bertie with it after they arrived there.

"Which throws up the million-dollar question—why did Bertie go with him so willingly?"

Supt. Matthews needed a break to gather his thoughts, so he took the afternoon off to play golf with former top jockey, Ian Watkinson, who had come to live in Aber Tidy from Newmarket, the country's leading racehorse centre.

Pressure was beginning to build on Matthews, so he grabbed the chance to whack the little white ball to get rid of the escalating frustration, and enjoyed a few hours of banter as they strolled in glorious summer sunshine.

When Supt Matthews returned to the incident room entirely refreshed, Lewis and Smith were copying out three sheets of A4-size paper containing a detailed report of their research into Bertie Brown's fascinating background…

It began… BERTIE BROWN was, ironically chairman

of the Aber Tidy archery club, president of Aber Tidy football club, treasurer of the local Conservative Club, enjoyed playing snooker and darts, and would have been 54 next Tuesday.

He owned a timeshare apartment in Tenerife, worshipped at St. Mary's, drove a year-old, top-range Land-Rover, and was appointed bank manager in 2015.

In addition, he played the piano "badly", generously supported the Doolally Valley orchestra, was never involved in controversial disputes, and was a "jolly good boss."

Lewis commented: "As far as we can tell, he didn't gamble, do drugs, or play away... So what did he do to displease someone so much that he was practically split in half?"

"So, there you have it!" droned Sgt Griffiths.

"Top guy, not an enemy in the world… Well, not quite. Whoever put an arrow through Bertie's heart didn't do it by accident, that's for sure.

"So, what are we missing? The killer has to be someone in the Valley. But who?"

Having presented Bertie Brown's biography with succinct clarity, Lewis and Smith caused a bit of a shock when they added that Dan Wood was also a long-standing member of the archery club.

Supt. Matthews leapt from his chair, and gasped, "I knew it! I knew it! He must be interviewed!"

With a cheeky grin, Smith then asked, "Would you like the names of every member of the archery club, sir?"

And before he had time to bellow, "Of course!" Smith was waving two sheets of A4 that contained every name, contact number, and email address.

"Well done, lads," applauded the impressed superintendent.

"Now, split the list between you, and interview every one of them, particularly focusing on any connection with Bertie Brown, and what they thought of him as a person, and bank manager.

"Remember, whoever you speak to is the potential murderer, so be alert, and use guile and discretion at all times, okay?"

Lewis and Smith divided the list, as instructed, and went their separate ways while Matthews and Griffiths returned to Dan Wood's home in Grace Road.

Dan Wood answered the doorbell, handsomely bronzed from his Lanzarote fortnight, and then led the officers to the comfy, red leather suite of sofas in the lounge.

Two hours of friendly chat ensued in which Dan Wood answered every question calmly, and politely, and repeatedly insisted that he and Bertie were good friends, and that he understood why Bertie had refused his request for a £50,000 loan, though it was "too personal" for him to elaborate.

There was no animosity between them, and he genuinely believed that Bertie was a far better bowman.

Matthews and Griffiths were now satisfied that Mr. Wood didn't come across as a killer, or even someone who would hire a killer, so he was finally dropped as a suspect.

Tom Morgan, gossipy manager of the Bell Hotel, was waiting for Matthews and Griffiths when they returned to the incident room with, what he believed, could be crucial information.

Producing an invoice from his pocket, Mr. Morgan excitedly said, "That man stayed at The Bell on the night before the murder. To be honest, he gave me the creeps.

"I tried to get him to chat, but all he said was 'I'm here on business!' He was in no mood to talk, so I said 'good night' and he didn't reply.

"He stood well over six feet, had a neat, pointed beard, and shot away in a red Ferrari just after nine in the morning."

Typed out on the crumpled hotel receipt was the name Giovanni Bonetti, leaving no-one in doubt about his Italian nationality.

Matthews and Griffiths thanked Mr. Morgan, and went straight to the CCTV footage, desperately hoping the red

Ferrari would appear somewhere so that they could note its registration plate, and track it out of town.

Their luck was in. Footage from Saturday morning showed the topless Ferrari parked outside the workingmen's club in Gough Street, with the towering Italian standing alongside it.

The mysterious Bonetti was in deep conversation with Roy Rogers, the Festival's chief sponsor, a wealthy house builder, and inevitably known as 'Cowboy', which he insisted had nothing to do with his quality of work.

Bonetti and Rogers chatted for around five minutes, and when their animated conversation ended with a firm handshake, the Italian clearly slipped a small package to Rogers, and then drove off at high speed over Harris Hill.

Sgt Griffiths was quick to notice that the registration plates had been removed, which made it plain that this was someone alert to CCTV cameras and, whatever his mission, he had no wish to be identified.

Supt. Matthews, bubbling and squeaking, predictably resurrected his hit-man' theory, and now thought that if Bonetti was not working for Dan Wood he could still have committed the murder for someone else.

Cadet Lewis, an extremely bright lad, who turned down university to enlist in the police Force straight from school, was already producing investigatory skills that made him a cast-iron favourite for forensic stardom

With Supt. Matthews still rattling on about a hit-man doing someone else's grisly work, Lewis raised a hand and advised everyone about the range and manufacture of crossbows.

Exuding remarkable confidence for someone so young, he warned: "With respect to everyone, I think we must be careful not to assume that all crossbows are large, expensive and, most importantly, made of wood.

"Crossbows can be bought for as little as £40 from traders on the Web, and are mainly made of plastic and aluminium, though the wood version is also available, and can cost up to £350.

“And they don’t need to be licensed or registered, but under UK law they must not be carried in public.

“So, provided you are over 18, you may purchase this lethal weapon, and go straight out and use it.”

Lewis then spoke about traditional target arrows, adding that Club 700 was the archery projectile, and generally cost around £7.00.

Before sitting at his desk, Lewis announced that he and Smith had met Stan Bolt, chairman of the archery club that boasted 23 members, and Mr. Bolt had confidentially given them the names of those he thought were skilled enough to commit the murder.

Lewis pinned a copy of the names to the information board in the incident room. Stan Bolt believed the six best bowmen for nerve and accuracy were…

Chris Thomas, 37, self-employed plumber.

Dan Wood, 53, self-employed carpenter.

Carlos Botti, 44, jeweller, orchestra viola leader.

Damien Brierley, 28, bets shop boss, darts champion

Ian Howgate, 53, financial adviser.

Hannah Gutteridge, 33, media consultant.

Supt. Matthews required personal checks on all of them, and again gave the task to Lewis and Smith.

TUESDAY, JUNE 19, 2018

By now, Sgt. Griffiths had met Stan Bolt at the forensic laboratory where the archery club chairman recognized the fatal arrow as one of the three that had vanished from his stock in the past six weeks.

This disclosure inevitably caused great alarm in the incident room, as it virtually confirmed that the killer was a club member, and likely to be in possession of the other missing missiles.

Sgt. Griffiths prompted Lewis and Smith to speed up their research before the killer had time to strike again.

Lewis and Smith had each taken three club members to scrutinize, and they increased inquiries to 12 hours a day, now setting off at 8.0am.

There was no respite for the overworked quartet, and certainly no time to relax at Aber Tidy's annual Music Extravaganza at the town hall on Saturday, July 7, except for the boss, of course.

Supt. Matthews convinced his team that this was the type of event where the killer could mix with the crowd to murder his second victim, just as he mixed with the crowd to slay Bertie Brown and, for this reason, he needed to be there.

It was a spooky prediction, and unusual for Matthews, as his general approach was to focus on the facts, while not allowing intuition and gut feelings to enter his thinking.

But this time he was going to be spot on. Indeed, the crossbow assassin could well have been finalizing his plans as the police chief made his unique chilling forecast.

Lewis eventually dared to ask him whether he possessed a crystal-ball at home, or was he, indeed, blessed with a massive psychic gift?

Again, it was an early morning dog-walker who came across the body in precisely the same area in Bluebell Woods where Bertie Brown was found murdered.

It was on its back and, just as before, an arrow was embedded in his heart, only this time the killer was in a rush, as no attempt had been made to cover the body with the heap of twigs and bracken that were spread all around it.

Matthews and Griffiths were soon on the scene, followed swiftly by Lewis and Smith, who were still gathering information on the six archery club suspects.

Once the forensic team had erected their mandatory security tent, a delicate search of the body found a wallet that contained a driving licence in the name of Andrew Black.

They also uncovered another chilling note in red capitals under a stone alongside the body…

Dr. Roger Owen recorded that Mr. Black, who owned a farm in Upper Doolally, had died between 8.15 and 9.0 the previous evening.

Supt. Matthews, bamboozled and infuriated, instructed his officers to "investigate like you've never investigated before."

With his voice at tenor pitch, he bellowed: "This is a

clever, ruthless killer, who walks among us, chats with us, laughs with us, but who the hell is he? Who the hell is Oliva?"

Matthews then turned to Lewis and Smith, and demanded: "You have 24 hours, and not a minute more, to complete your inquiries into the suspects.

"Detailed reports on all six must be on my desk by five o'clock tomorrow afternoon. So be off, and good luck."

There were now eight officers working on the case, and it was crucial that they remained calm, kept a clear head, and concentrated hard on finding clues, a practice they had all rehearsed many times at police training camps to prepare for such a challenge.

Supt. Matthews was back on his feet… "We're in the dark on this. We have no substantial clue, except for the missiles, which have offered no fingerprints, and we have no idea of the motive.

"Come on! Come on! We must do better!"

Sgt Griffiths burst into the room after an hour with Andrew Black's family. WPC Thomas had again been with him, and again stayed behind.

Black lived at Trafle Farm with his wife, Jean, and teenage sons, Geoffrey and Gwilym.

"Jean couldn't recall a single occasion when Andrew had had a fall-out with anyone," reported Sgt. Griffiths.

"He had no enemies. He was a popular guy. She's baffled and devastated.

"For five years, until 2016, he was a director of Aber Tidy football club, and enjoyed weekend trips with his mates to watch matches in Europe.

"He was one of 12 who'd been to Paris, Naples, Barcelona, and Madrid, plus a few other European cities that Jean couldn't recall.

"She also said, and this could be helpful, that Bertie Brown rarely missed a trip. Two murders and both victims went on weekend trips to watch football in Europe in a group of 12.

"Coincidence? Or connection? This could be the

breakthrough. So, let's work at it.

"Andrew Black's savings account was also at Bertie's bank. Again, coincidence or connection?"

It was around 4.30pm when Lewis and Smith returned with what they had discovered about the six specialist bowmen, importantly bringing news of where they were at the time of Andrew Black's murder.

Standing alongside the incident board, Lewis began with background information on archery club chairman, STAN BOLT…

"Mr. Bolt is 54, and married to Suzy. They have two daughters, and he's a member of the golf club, Bridge Club, vice-chairman of the Conservative Club, drives a year-old Mercedes, and never misses a local concert. He was in the town hall listening to the orchestra on the night Andrew Black was murdered. He knew Andrew to say 'good day' to, but no more than that."

"Now I come to CHRISTOPHER THOMAS, self-employed plumber, and still playing Sunday football for Royal Oak Rovers at 37 years of age. Current snooker league champion, and saves all his money, wait for it, at Bertie Brown's bank. Club archery champion for the past two years, and was drinking with friends at the Royal Oak on the night of the murder.

"Right, onto DAN WOOD, self-employed carpenter, and a highly skilled bowman who was runner-up in the annual Valley event in 2016. He's also a former Aber Tidy FC director, banked with Bertie Brown, and is one of the group who skip off to the continent to watch football etc. Insists he was at home watching TV with his family at the time of Andrew Black's murder, and holidaying in Lanzarote when Bertie Brown was killed.

"Next is CARLOS BOTTI. He's 44, and a wealthy jeweller. Came to Aber Tidy five years ago when he married Maggie Phillips, a dental assistant from Aberdare. He said he grew up in Milan, where he studied music. He's the orchestra's lead viola player. An archer with an additional bow, you might say! Hobbies include foreign travel, river fishing and opera, He was in the orchestra at the time of both murders. A strong archery competitor, who needs steady hands to play his viola. He also banked with Bertie Brown."

Lewis closed his blue folder and, as he sat alongside Sgt Griffiths, he whispered, "They are my three," and gesticulated to Smith to replace him at the front.

Smartly dressed in a navy blue, pinstriped suit, Smith looked the ultimate professional businessman. He towered from a height of 6ft 5in, and said, "I begin with the highly interesting DAMIEN BRIERLEY, currently in the top five of the Valley's darts league, and a world championship contestant in 2015.

"He's the ultimate Mr. Calm, with a vital firm hand, consistently focused, accurate, and a skilled bowman.

"He's 28, a passionate Coventry City football fan, a popular betting shop manager, drives a high-powered red BMW, and was competing in a darts league match at the Cross Keyes pub when Mr. Black was murdered. I should mention that the Cross Keys is barely 200 yards from Bluebell Woods. He knew Mr. Black well, having spent time with him on the football trips.

"Onto IAN HOWGATE, a busy financial adviser, and a strong campaigner for justice and fair play. Has worked tirelessly to help the homeless. Highly rated as a bowman. Can be fiery. Married with a teenage son, and teenage daughter. Banked with Bertie Brown. He's an athletic 52, and still plays an occasional game of league hockey.

"Finally, we have the elegant HANNAH GUTTERIDGE, a bright, efficient media consultant. League's leading lady bowman. Confident and decisive...But has as much chance of being a crossbow killer as playing full-back for Wales.

"That's my lot. Thank you."

Lewis and Smith had provided copies of the names to Supt. Matthews before they spoke, so he instantly launched into action, fussing around like his dear elderly granny until he had gathered all the required documents together, and finally stopped, and spoke to the officers.

“So, leaving out Hannah, we have five people to consider,” he said, virtually licking his lips.

“It’s a damn good start, but it’s no guarantee, so still be aware of anything suspicious you see or hear outside this group. But my money is on one of these five. Any takers?”

No-one dared challenge the superintendent. If he placed a bet that it would snow in August, it would snow in August!

He was now practically banned from the police social club after winning the bingo bonanza three Sundays in a row.

Then he tempted Lewis and Smith to name their five suspects in order of probability.

Lewis responded, “We’ve discussed it, sir, and we have that list.”

“Well done! Well done!” applauded Matthews.

Reading from his notebook, Lewis said: “Smith and I have Damien Brierley at the top. He’s a cool dude. He needs nerve and accuracy to be a darts champion. We think he might have a penchant for missiles.”

Matthews looked up sharply, “Big word, boy. Educated are you?”

Lewis totally blanked him, and went on, ”Then we have Ian Howgate, who’s something of a finance wizard, and a passionate campaigner for homeless people, and people sleeping rough. He’s strong, athletic, and positive. Can’t be ruled out.

“Dan Wood would certainly be a lively suspect if he’d not been on holiday, though a hit-man, I suppose, could have done it for him, but highly unlikely.

“There’s nothing to suggest that it’s Christopher Thomas or Carlos Botti, and we’ve already ruled out Hannah.”

Matthews appreciated the sterling work done by Lewis and Smith, but again reminded everyone that time was rushing by, and that they still had no motive or weapon to consider.

He asked: “Why have two such fine and popular

gentlemen been so brutally killed in a town where the biggest rows usually come at W.I. meetings over who's baked the best cream cakes?

"And how does the killer manage to carry the crossbow without it being seen? What are we missing?

"And let's not forget the killer's signature 'Oliva'. Do let me have your thoughts, please."

In absolute secrecy, Lewis and Smith were conducting their own private investigation into the murders, using all the information that was being collated in the incident room and, most importantly, sharing their thoughts with close friend Zach Jennings, a university criminology student.

They met every Sunday afternoon for a detailed discussion at Lewis' top floor apartment before Zach drove back to his lodgings where he listened to endless hours of classical music, especially Mozart.

Now, the committed trio was able to focus on five suspects to seek a motive, explain 'Oliva', work out how the killer concealed the crossbow, what linked the two victims, and ponder about a possible third murder, bearing in mind that three arrows had gone missing from the Archery club.

Lewis and Smith had returned to squeeze a bit more out of Andrew Black's family, in particular to establish whether he had had any social contact with Bertie Brown besides his business discussions at the bank.

Andrew's shattered wife, Jean, recalled there was just one occasion when Andrew and Bertie were among the Valley football group on a weekend trip to Italy.

She vividly remembered them being in Naples for three days, and she took a photograph from a desk drawer, which showed them all drinking and laughing outside a bar.

Smith quickly pointed to suspect Damien Brierley, smartly kitted out in a Coventry City sky-blue top, and raising a pint glass alongside his betting shop colleague, Ian Bremner, who was recording their antics on a video-camera that he had specially bought for the trip.

Smith counted out 12 in the photograph that showed Bertie Brown and Andrew Black chatting freely to an Italian policeman.

Jean happily let Smith take the photograph back to the station on the strict promise that he would return it once it had been copied.

Supt. Matthews was ecstatic on seeing the photograph, and regarded it as “another major step forward.”

Lewis and Smith, of course, couldn’t wait to produce it at their next meeting with Zach.

Constable Brian J. Lee was given the tedious job of finding people who could put names to the faces in the photograph, which took him a week.

Heads were firmly down, scrutinizing documents, and examining yet more CCTV footage, especially of the days leading up to both murders, when Sgt Griffiths burst through the door, waving a large, brown jiffy bag, and calling out, “Stop! Stop everything!”

Supt. Matthews hurried from his desk and watched closely as Sgt Griffiths carefully took two small audio cassettes out of the bag.

Every officer gathered at the table while Sgt Griffiths placed a high-tech tape-recorder in front of them. The room was eerily silent in nervous expectation.

Supt. Matthews held up the jiffy bag, and said: “Before we play the tapes, I should like to show you that this bag was addressed…

“And, as you can see, it’s in red ink again, and in the same thick capital letters. Yes, and it’s signed ‘OLIVA’.

“This guy is taunting us… He’s bloody taunting us!

“Our first job now is to play these cassettes, and I urge you all to listen carefully, really, really carefully, and miss nothing!”

Sgt Griffiths had already inserted the first cassette, and pressed the button immediately Supt. Matthews gave a positive nod.

The response was instant... A soft voice, with an exaggerated North Wales accent, warned...

There was absolute silence. Blank faces and rolling eyes exposed the extreme concern at this scary message.

Supt. Matthews said there would be no discussion until they'd moved on and heard the second cassette.

Sgt Griffiths again pressed the button, and the same weird Welsh voice droned...

Sgt Griffiths then addressed the stunned and riveted officers…"Before we examine what we've just heard, I should like to make clear that the jiffy bag was handed to an officer on the station steps by a guy dressed in black leathers, and riding a powerful motor-cycle, who roared off at top speed towards Swansea."

Every officer was advised to take an hour's break while that day's CCTV footage was collected from Joe Grierson at County Hall.

Supt. Matthews grabbed the chance to hurry home to meet Brighton architect, Max Wooton, who had arranged a visit to plan a conservatory that would join directly onto the dining-room.

Aber Tidy builder, Pete Chapman, an Arsenal addict, had recommended the former Bournemouth Arts University student, having worked with him on many successful projects.

Meanwhile, despite the dramatic developments, Sgt. Griffiths remained calm, and told his team: "We will look first at how these cassettes were delivered to us, and by whom.

"CCTV footage from the four High Street cameras will take priority. Look closely at the rider and the bike. Note its plates! The model!

"It's broad daylight, for heaven's sake. I can't believe he risked being seen."

Lewis and Smith were instructed to peruse every single frame of the footage and to question anything that seemed remotely suspicious.

Smith was a huge superbike follower, who rarely missed the annual Isle of Man TT races, so quite easily identified it as an Italian top-of-the-range Ducati, from a factory in Bolognia.

Before leaving the station, Smith and Lewis collected a copy of both cassettes to play in a quiet corner at home, and put in front of Zach.

The two original cassettes were rushed to the Aber Tidy police laboratory where newly installed equipment could tell whether an accent was genuine or disguised.

In this case, the answer seemed obvious, as the North Wales accent sounded far too strong to be real, and after 30 minutes of close analysis, the technicians confirmed that that was the case.

Matthews and Griffiths wondered whether the killer would take such a big chance of being seen, or was it more likely to be a close friend, or even an associate in the murders.

Well, definitely not Dai 'twp' Richards," joked Matthews. "He'd have a problem staying on a child's three-wheeler."

Matthews was dubious and cautious, but he had to concede that the killer must have been involved in some way, if not entirely, because who else would have known about Oliva, and the printed red capitals?

Literally speaking to himself, which he did quite often, and claimed it was always an intelligent debate, Matthews muttered, "If this was not the killer, maybe he shares a house with someone who has a motor-bike or, indeed, there might be two people working together.

"Questions! Questions! Questions! Time and time again, it's a question. Is it this? Or is it that? I'm tired of it. What we need are answers, and fast!

"Can someone please arrange for Poirot, Jack Frost, Vera, Morse, Perry Mason, and even Miss Marple to join us, and she can bring along her knitting."

"And Colombo," chipped in Lewis. "And we can buy him a new raincoat, and a decent car!"

It generated refreshing laughter.

Matthews then decided to bring in Mystic Megan Thomas, the valley's popular fortune-teller, who had helped Aber Tidy police solve many tricky cases.

Mystic Megan was a former Amman Valley line-dancing champion along with her light-footed husband, Irfon, who ran the L-Passo driving school.

Megan apologized for arriving late, having been delayed by council chairman, Mansel Thomas, who had pleaded with her to read his tealeaves and advise him on his future, as he nervously prepared for his fourth marriage in ten years.

Supt. Matthews came off the phone holding his hand to his mouth and rocking with laughter.

After finally calming down, he chuckled, "That was Dai 'twp' Richards advising me that he'd seen a notice in the window of that new shop in Garw Road that said 'Ties just £2' and insisted they'd come from Bangkok, capital of Tieland!

"I didn't have the heart to tell him that it's the new dry-cleaning business, and that jackets and trousers were just £5.00, as well!"

Lewis and Smith welcomed Zach to the apartment, and they listened closely to the cassettes that were repeatedly played at different speeds and different volume.

It was while enjoying a well-earned beer and a ham sandwich that Zach said… "Do you know, I'm sure I heard an orchestra playing in the background on the first cassette. Can I hear it again, please?"

Lewis promptly put the cassette back in the machine while Zach placed his ear close to the speaker, and gasped, "Yes, yes! There it is! Stop! Play it back!"

Lewis did what was requested, and then all three listened closely, but it was only Zach who could actually pick out the music.

With a finger to his lips, Zach whispered: "I can hear an orchestra. And I'm pretty sure it's playing the Thieving Magpie overture… Yes, it's the Thieving Magpie…"

And he whistled it loudly, and Lewis and Smith recognized it and joined in.

The talented trio then focused on what was said on the tapes, and played them over and over again.

They listened first to the one that referred to Bluebell Woods, and Lewis concluded that this was the killer, and that he'd got to know that two CCTV cameras had been secretly installed high above where the two murders had been committed.

"Let's hear it again," said Lewis, and it played...

'Bluebell Woods will be no more;

'I'm moving closer to the shore...'

"But what shore?" wondered Lewis. "Porthcawl, Aberavon, Barry Island? It's a wide area. We shall have to narrow it down."

Zach chipped in: "Can we now look at the photograph of those guys on a weekend somewhere in Italy?"

"Naples!" said Lewis. "It's a great picture. Every face is clear. And we can now put names to them all."

"So, is there one who lives near the shore?" asked Zach.

"There are two, and both in Barry Island," answered Lewis.

"Mark Piel, a betting shop colleague of Damien Brierley and Ian Bremner, and Mike Harris, boss of Harris Coaches.

"Both are ordinary guys, who enjoy a few beers and a couple of nights abroad with their mates.

"There are just 25 miles between Barry Island and Aber Tidy, so it's a straightforward drive to work. No hassle."

Zach was in a deep, contemplative mood, with his head in his hands. He was full of thought...

"What's up?" snapped Lewis.

"I think a picture could be developing," Zach replied.

"It's possible. Just possible No more than that! There's still a lot of work to be done. Now, I must be off..."

WEDNESDAY, AUGUST 8, 2018.

Lewis was plainly bothered, and groaned: "I didn't sleep a wink. Couldn't get the thought of a third murder out of my mind.

"I kept mulling over who might be the next victim, and why, but got nowhere, except to rule out Mark Piel and Michael Harris.

"The killer already knows exactly where and when he will do it. There's so much confidence. He has no thought of getting caught.

"If we don't nail him soon we'll have more dead bodies than Midsomer Murders!"

Supt. Matthews had pinned a report to the Incident Board that he had just received from the Voice Testing Laboratory…

Dear Supt. Matthews,
After several hours of examining the two 'Crossbow' cassettes on high quality voice identification equipment, our findings are given below…

As you know, the voice on both cassettes was male, and we concluded that it contained the depth of resonance that can be safely assumed was someone aged between 35 and 55.

What we had to establish was whether it was a genuine North Wales accent, or one that was being contrived to sound like one.

Every test left us in no doubt that it was not a natural North Wales accent. We couldn't be exact on what it was, but we hope that by gauging the age, this will help you eliminate anyone outside this range.

Good luck and best wishes,
John Deacon
Manager,
Voice-testing Laboratory,
Doolally Valley.

Lewis, Smith and Zach were whacked by the end of their long session. Of course, they had no say on policy, but their sharp minds, strong intuition, and a fervent wish to catch the killer put them level with everyone else on the case, bearing in mind that they had access to all relevant information.

A police handwriting expert was on her way from Bridgend to analyse the printing on the jiffy bag, which had mysteriously vanished overnight.

Matthews and Griffiths blamed each other for its disappearance in what would have been a riotous sketch if the situation wasn't so serious.

Smith eventually raised his arm to stop the pantomime, and told his bosses, "All is fine! Look!" And he casually took the jiffy bag from his personal locker, and explained: "I saw it lying on the table when we left last night, and I was worried the cleaners might think it was rubbish, so I put it somewhere safe…"

Huge Chelsea supporter Kathy Seymour, softly-spoken, and with attractive streaks of pink and blue in her hair, peered through her brand new rimless spectacles at the red printing on the jiffy bag.

Matthews and Griffiths pulled up chairs to sit each side of her, desperately hoping that a sizeable clue was about to emerge.

Having listened to the cassettes umpteen times, and virtually satisfied themselves that it was the killer's disguised voice, Matthews and Griffiths oozed optimism as Kathy meticulously examined the bag in which they arrived.

Within a minute she concluded that whoever addressed the bag had cunningly used his 'wrong' hand to print the individual letters.

Kathy explained: "A natural right-hander has used his left hand, or the other way round. That's why the letters look as though they've been done by someone heavily intoxicated or in his nineties.

"I should like to take copies away with me to examine

at home, and I'll email a full report in the next few days."

Matthews and Griffiths thanked Kathy for her expertise, and while she was being escorted from the station, a full conference was called of every officer on the case to review their progress.

High on the list was the red Ferrari and its mysterious driver filmed speaking to Roy Rogers, the Festival sponsor, and seemingly slipping something into his hand.

Sgt. Griffiths revealed that CCTV cameras had spotted the car boarding a ferry in Dover that was sailing to Calais.

French police readily agreed to trace it, but the ferry had arrived, and all vehicles had rolled off before the request had reached them.

Nevertheless, they committed themselves to treating it as an emergency, and launched a nationwide search, and engaged Interpol.

Cassettes, jiffy bag, arrows used in the killings, and a whole host of other items were reviewed in specific detail, inevitably concluding with the 'message' to prepare for a third murder, which would not be committed in Bluebell Woods.

After three hours of intense debate, broken up only for refreshments and comfort trips down the corridor, Supt. Matthews got to his feet, and addressed every single one of them with a voice that trembled from escalating concern.

He began: "It feels like we're waiting for a time-bomb to explode. Where? When? Who? We have five positive suspects. We must go through each one again. Microscopically. Everyone one of them must be interviewed immediately.

"Smith you take Howgate; Sgt Griffiths will take Botti; I'll see Wood; Lewis will call on Thomas, and Sgt Roy Evans will call on Brierley.

"We'll start tomorrow. Sleep well."

It was 9.15 pm and not a single officer headed to a pub. Driving straight home was a priority. Preparation was vital for their key visits.

Supt. Matthews was literally crawling under the covers

when the telephone rang on his bedside table.

It was duty station officer Paul Bryant with devastating information. The killer had struck again.

All Sgt. Bryant could tell the boss was that a motorist had rung in from a lay-by on the Aber Tidy to Barry Island road, to say that a male body was lying in the bushes with an arrow stuck in his back.

Matthews and Griffiths were first on the scene, and were met by a male body, face down, spread-eagled in the hedge, and with an archery club arrow in the middle of his back that glistened in the midnight moonlight.

A white 'A' class Mercedes, with personalized plates, was parked in the lay-by, which meant that Matthews knew immediately that Roy Rogers was lying prostrate in front of him.

Rogers, aged 53, was a divorced, self-employed builder, Festival chairman, cricket club president, freelance violinist, and a regular member of the Valley's foreign football trips squad.

Dr. Owen timed the murder at 8.00pm in broad daylight, and concluded that the angle of the arrow indicated that it had been fired around 30 yards from the opposite side of the road.

Supt. Matthews instructed his officers to return to the incident-room, while two detectives remained at the crime scene with forensic experts, a pathologist, and Dr. Owen, who had removed a white sheet of paper sticking out of Rogers' trousers pocket.

Printed in the now familiar red capitals were the words…

Griffiths groaned, “Not exactly Wordsworth, but he certainly knows how to write a frightening message.”

That evening, Matthews had been invited as guest speaker at the annual golf club dinner, which he welcomed as a massive relief from the mind busting pressure.

When the time came to stand up, he thanked Tom Thomas for the “delicious Welsh beef” that filled his plate, and praised Mandy Dennis for the “enormous help” she was providing as chair lady of Neighbourhood Watch.

He also couldn’t resist launching into two of his favourite gags that produced side-splitting laughter.

I make no apologies for recalling them here. With professional timing and polished delivery, the exuberant Matthews said…

“Burglar Nick Silver broke into the big house on the hill shortly after midnight. It was pitch black as he crept around the lounge.

“Suddenly, he heard a voice coming from the far corner of the room that said, ‘Be careful, Jesus is watching you. He’s watching you very closely.’

“When Nick Silver reached the dark corner he found a parrot in a cage, and he asked, ‘Was it you who said Jesus was watching me?’

“’Yes, that was me,’ replied the parrot.

“What’s your name?” asked Nick Silver.

“’It’s Ebonezer,’” replied the parrot.

“What idiot gave you a daft name like that?” asked Nick Silver.

‘The same idiot that named the rotweiller Jesus!’ chuckled the parrot.

Matthews raised his hand to end the loud laughter so that he could continue with his second gag. He said…

“The Duke of Norfolk came to Doolally Valley to see his horse, Bolt Up, run in the Aber Tidy Derby, and while walking to the paddock he saw the trainer slip something into the horse’s mouth.

“’Excuse me,’” said the Duke, “’what was that you were giving to my horse?’”

“’Absolutely harmless, my Lord,’” replied the trainer.

“’Look, you have one, and I’ll have one.’”

“The Duke swallowed it on the spot, and hurried back to the grandstand to watch the race.

“Meanwhile, the trainer was heard to say to his jockey, ‘Hold him up to the two-furlong pole and then let him go, and if anyone passes you it will either be me or the Duke of Norfolk!’”

Matthews beamed in response to a blast of tumultuous laughter, and calmly sat down. His job was done. He felt a million miles away from his criminal investigation, and was relaxed, refreshed, and rejuvenated.

Sadly, it lasted less than 12 hours before he was back in the morass of murder and a frantic killer hunt.

THURSDAY, AUGUST 16, 2018

Literally, as he opened his office door, the abnormally loud desk telephone greeted him before he had time to take his jacket off. It was 7.58am.

He took the call standing up, but was quickly sitting down, his face ashen, and his head swinging loosely from side to side.

Archery club chairman Stan Bolt was on the line with the alarming news that a fourth arrow had now vanished from the club.

Matthews was speechless. A serial killer was strolling the streets, browsing in shop windows, inevitably drinking in the The Bell or Royal Oak, and having a jolly good laugh at the police scrambling around in the dark. He was furious.

Griffiths came through the door unaware of the latest missing arrow, but not for long, as Matthews frantically spluttered it out. They gasped in unison.

Matthews demanded to see the photograph of the group in Naples, confident that Roy Rogers was among them.

And he swiftly recalled the red Ferrari, and the mystery driver slipping something into Rogers' hand before being caught on CCTV boarding a ferry at Dover back to the continent.

Griffiths just couldn't understand why Rogers had clearly agreed to meet the killer in a lay-by on a main road when The Bell Inn would have been far more comfortable.

"What is the common link?" barked Griffiths. "There has to be a link. These are not random murders. They are brutal killings for a reason. A massive reason! But what is it?"

Lewis and Smith returned to the station shortly after 3.30 pm, having completed their crucial interviews, and went straight into them.

Supt Matthews suddenly bawled "Eureka!" having found that Oliva was a small Spanish town in the province of Valencia, but had absolutely no idea where it fitted in.

Smith then confirmed that Roy Rogers was in the Naples photograph, slightly obscured by Bertie Brown, while he and Andrew Black were speaking to the Italian police officer.

Biggest worry now was finding, and alerting, whoever the killer had in mind as his next victim.

Lewis emerged from Legends, the Valley's busiest hairdressing saloon, where award-winning stylist, Suzanne, had maximized her scissors skills to transform him into a reasonably handsome investigator.

It was a pity nothing could be done to straighten his offensive nose that was bent in a brawl in a hostile rugby match for Aber Tidy Rovers, which they lost.

An early-morning text message to Zach's posh mobile was his main priority to ask if all three could meet in Aber Tidy next day to discuss the increasing fear of a fourth murder.

Zach had no pressing lectures scheduled until the following Tuesday, so he arrived at Lewis' apartment early on Friday and stayed the weekend.

Supt. Matthews announced that Roy Rogers, like Andrew Black, also banked with Bertie Brown, and wondered whether this was worth investigating.

FRIDAY, AUGUST 24, 2018.

Lewis called it Judgment Day.
Zach arrived at 9.30 a.m.

Lewis and Smith cheekily invited Matthews and Griffiths to join them in a full-scale forensic breakdown of the baffling case.

They arrived together at 10.35 a.m., carrying the entire case file.

Lewis introduced Zach as an "above average university criminology student", and then all five sat around the large circular table, with Matthews, understandably, taking the role of chairman.

For simplicity it was agreed that they would proceed chronologically, and Matthews set the proverbial ball rolling…

He began: "The weekend in Naples, it seems, would be a good place to kick-off. A suitable football phrase, you might say…

"Three people in a photograph of the group on that Italian weekend have been murdered in a matter of weeks.

"I refuse to accept it was mere coincidence. Rubbish! It's connected! I'm sure of it. Do we all agree?"

A resounding 'yes' echoed around the table. Unanimity from the outset…

Lewis referred specifically to that weekend of February 10, recalling that the group had watched Napoli win 4-1 in an Italian League match.

A list of crucial questions had been drawn up by Lewis regarding that Naples visit, all aimed at uncovering, what was now unanimously agreed, the root cause of the killings…

What were Rogers, Black, and Brown discussing with the police officer?

Was the killer one of the group?

Were other helpful photographs available?

Was it time to contact the video cameraman?

Supt. Matthews wired the police officer's photograph to his Naples headquarters, asking for him to contact the murder inquiry team urgently.

But he was out of the country on holiday, and would ring on his return in five days.

Should the killer be in the group, Damien Brierley was the only suspect because of his archery club connection but, at 28, he didn't fit the 35 to 55 age range.

Zach chipped in: "I'm ruling him out. There is someone far more likely."

"What!" Griffiths gasped. "Are you seriously saying you have a prime suspect?"

"Yes," replied Zach. "But I'd rather wait until we've got answers to a few more questions."

There was a ten-second silence as the shocked officers just looked blank at one another, totally lost for words.

"All right," said Matthews, "what questions do you have in mind?"

Not wishing to over-excite the bosses, Zach replied calmly, "If my theory is right, I should like you, sir, or Sgt Griffiths, to return to the bank and check through the personal accounts of Brown, Black and Rogers for any suspicious payments."

Griffiths immediately volunteered, and politely rang deputy manager, Allan Mercado, to ask for these personal accounts to be ready when he arrived in the next ten to 15 minutes.

Griffiths returned in less than an hour with incredible information.

Zach greeted him: "Well, what did you find?"

Griffiths: "Amazing! Astonishing! Settle down everyone, and listen to this…

"Murder victims Brown and Black had each put £5,000 into their accounts in the first week of every month since March, and Rogers had put in £20,000 in one go last month.

"It was all cash. There was no hint of where it came

from. Not a clue…"

"Pretty obvious, though," slipped in Matthews.

"They were being paid to keep their mouths shut. It was blackmail. And the paymaster finished them off."

Zach nodded, and confirmed: "Correct. Now we move on. Remember, there is still a missing, unused arrow from the club. Someone's name is on that one…"

Matthews: "Any idea who that might be?"

Zach: "It can only be one. And, if I'm right, he wasn't a blackmailer, and he didn't bank with Bertie…

"I think Ian Bremner should be given maximum protection. But done cleverly. To catch the killer we must not show out!"

All five fell into shocked silence, as they digested what had been fed to them, and then chewed over what was to come, and why it could be Bremner.

"So, who the hell is it?" Sgt Griffiths bellowed in raging frustration.

"Calm yourself," pleaded Zach, as he took an A-4 size wall poster out of his over-loaded brief-case…

It was a colourful reminder of Lady Liddiard's annual garden party at the Tree House on Saturday, September 8, and listed the entertainment, and promised the usual succulent strawberries and cream.

At this point, Zach got to his feet and asked Supt. Matthews to play the footage recorded on the CCTV camera that covered the Green on the day Bertie Brown was murdered.

"Will do!" responded Matthews, who quickly produced the relevant reel, and was poised to begin, having no idea what Zach had in mind.

Stepping forward, Zach explained: "I'd like to see footage of the orchestra returning to the bandstand after their 30-minute break…"

Supt. Matthews did exactly what Zach requested, and tension mounted as everyone realized that the proverbial bomb was about to explode.

Zach suddenly said: "Stop! Stop right there! Now look

closely. The orchestra has begun playing, but what do you see at the end of the second row on the right?"

"An empty chair," they chorused.

"Keep watching," said Zach.

"Now, what do you see?"

"Carlos Botti going towards the vacant seat," said Smith.

"And what is he carrying?" continued Zach.

"A viola case," said Lewis and Smith together.

"And what does he do with it?" asked Zach.

"He's putting it down…alongside another one," gasped Lewis.

"Correct," praised Zach. "But which one does he take his viola out of?

"The one that was already there," enthused Supt. Matthews.

"Which leaves us wondering what was in the one that he brought onto the bandstand after the interval… Would anyone like to guess?"

Zach was being cheeky now, but no-one cared a bit. This was a stupendous result.

Sgt Griffiths chimed in, "So that's how he managed to conceal the crossbow. He hid it in a viola case… And it fitted perfectly. That's truly fantastic, Zach."

Supt. Matthews needed five minutes to regain his composure after such a seismic shock.

"We need to plan carefully and discreetly," he advised, very much stating the obvious.

"Botti will be placed under intense 24-hour observation. Every move will be witnessed, photographed, and recorded. Discretion is imperative.

"We will carry on doing our inquiries in the usual way. Nothing changes. No excitement. Just plod on until we nail him…"

"When?" asked Griffiths.

Smith responded: "Lady Liddiard is a big classical music fan, and she invites a reduced orchestra to play at her fete every year, and Botti never misses."

Yet more disturbing news came from Lewis, who said a 'For Sale' board had been hammered into Botti's front lawn, and a neighbour had said that the jewellery shop was being handed over to his brother, Luca, who owned the highly acclaimed Valle d'Oro restaurant in Gough Square.

A worried Lewis added: "He's returning to his family in Italy. He's all set to go. We need to act fast."

Raising a hand, Zach said: "Calm it! Slow it down! He's going nowhere until he eliminates Bremner.

"Let me explain. Bremner's been too frightened to blackmail him, but remember what he was carrying when that vital picture was taken…"

"Video-camera!" snapped Smith. "And whatever is behind this mystery will have been recorded. Bremner will have the lot on tape. Evidence. Immense evidence."

"Correct," said Zach, who continued: "Bremner needs round-the-clock protection. He's vulnerable. Though Botti will probably wait until Lady Liddiard's fete before pulling the string. That's when Bremner will require priority protection."

Zach knew that this was a perfect time to clear up the many loose ends, and said, "First, the red Ferrari and mystery Italian called Bonetti who was caught on camera heading to Spain…"

"Go on," urged Matthews.

"Thank you," replied Zach, who commanded a captive audience, desperate for clarification.

He went on: "You'll all remember that Bonetti was caught on CCTV slipping something into Roy Rogers' hand. Well, take it from me that was his £20,000 lump sum.

"He was catching up. He'd not taken it monthly, like Bertie and Black."

Lewis then took over, announcing that he'd checked on the mystery motor-bike, and found that it was a Ducati, exactly what Snith had said, and that it was hired from Morgan Morgan Motors by Botti's brother, Luca, who would soon be running the jewellery business.

It was agreed that a small team of officers disguised in civilian clothes, would keep Botti under observation right up to Lady Liddiard's garden party.

Enormous tension grew daily as plans were put in place for the crucial arrest, when timing had to be precise, and nothing could afford to go wrong.

Bremner was taken to Lewis' apartment and slowly briefed on what he had to do to ensure the project worked and Botti was nailed in the act.

Most important of all, of course, was to ensure that Botti didn't slay him while undercover officers were getting into position on the lawn.

Botti had already been on the phone to Bremner and invited him to meet a short distance from Lady Liddiard's lawn, down the hill, behind the church.

He suggested that they met while the orchestra was on its 30-minute break.

Supt. Matthews instructed Bremner to comply with everything Botti requested, and to remain chatty and calm should they speak again on the phone.

However, on no account must he walk down the hill exposing his back to Botti, who had less than 50 yards to walk from the garden to a large blackberry bush from where he would be hidden, and could take aim at a clear target.

SATURDAY, SEPTEMBER 8, 2018.

Hot and sunny from daybreak… By early afternoon the temperature had soared to 23 degrees, and male guests started to gather in smart, open-necked shirts, and the ladies in long, flowery cotton dresses, shaded by a colourful mix of impressive headwear.

Lady Liddiard greeted everyone cheerfully at the main gate, shrewdly protected by a massive pink hat with a wide brim that had 'Ascot' written all over it.

Lord Speen was one of the first to arrive, having driven 110 miles up the M4 from Newbury in Berkshire.

Hampshire cricket guru Chris Miller, and his two talented sons, Mark and Roger, had driven specially from Southampton, and Aber Tidy's own cricket legend, Morley Howell, had also arrived early.

Lady Liddiard had been a big cricket fan since living in the same Essex street as a famous England batsman, who provided free tickets for her to watch Test matches at Lord's.

Dan Wood was another early guest, but swiftly turned his head when Supt Matthews strolled in wearing a pair of light brown shorts that you'd more likely associate with a Boy Scouts jamboree and, quite frankly, had taken disguise to a ludicrous level.

As expected, the orchestra had been trimmed to 12 players to fit comfortably on the lawn, and Botti had again positioned himself at the end of the second row where it would be simple for him to slip behind the house, through the gate, and down the hill.

Two viola cases could be seen placed beside his seat, one slightly larger than the other, but no-one took a second glance.

Everyone was too busy nattering, and cooling themselves with a vast choice of liquid refreshments kindly provided in bottles and cans.

It was the Valley's principal social event which, in less than an hour, would be transformed into a dramatic movie scene that Lady Liddiard knew all about, but was following police instructions to claim that it had come as a surprise.

Every move had been meticulously prepared. Everyone was in place. Lewis, Smith and Zach sat on folding chairs close to the orchestra, while Matthews and Griffiths mingled and chatted, but with their eyes rigidly focused on Botti as the first half ended with a Mozart overture requested by Lady Liddiard.

Two detectives were waiting for Botti near the blackberry bush where it was thought he would fire the arrow into Bremner's back as he walked down the hill.

Botti approached them briskly, carrying a black viola case. He had no time to waste.

"Good afternoon, gentlemen," he said politely, with a lingering smile.

"Good afternoon," responded the officers.

"Going the wrong way to make music aren't you?" said Sergeant David Willetts, and stepped in front of Botti, completely blocking his way on the narrow path.

As planned, Matthews and Griffiths came casually on the scene, and stood right behind Botti to make sure he couldn't turn and run. He was pinned in.

And while he protested, and frantically tried to break free, Griffiths flexed his muscles, barged his way forward, grabbed the case, and said, "I think I'll take that and make a bit of music. What do you say, Mr. Botti?"

The Italian musician was anchored to the spot. Lewis, Smith and Zach had now joined the melee, and Matthews pulled Botti's wrists together, slapped on a pair of silver handcuffs, and rejoiced, "The curtain's come down on you, maestro. Your fiddling days are done."

There was no surprise when Griffiths prised open the case to reveal a wooden crossbow, an arrow, and a note in red capital letters on a white sheet of paper, which he rammed into his pocket without even looking at it.

Having bundled Botti into a police van, Matthews, Griffiths, Lewis, Smith and Zach filled a separate car and headed to the apartment that had virtually become their headquarters.

Order had now been restored on the lawn, and the orchestra had resumed its programme. Lewis rolled down the car window to listen to them playing.

Incredibly, it was the William Tell overture by the prolific Italian composer Rossini, a legendary folklore story about a heroic Swiss crossbow marksman.

"Well, well, well," chuckled Zach. "What a coincidence!"

"Maybe they knew," joked Smith.

Bremner joined the five at Lewis' apartment, and they all grabbed a can of lager, and toasted their success.

But Matthews was not finished yet, and he said to Bremner: "You were clearly today's target because you video-recorded something of great importance in Naples. Well, what was it?"

Drawing a chair to the table, Bremner finally revealed what had caused the three gruesome murders.

"It was like this... Bertie, Andrew, and Roy were fancying some nice Italian shirts in a shop window, when Roy turned round and saw Botti standing on the opposite side of the road, and called him over.

"He said he was visiting friends in Naples, and that he'd be taking a train back to his home in Milan later that evening. He said it was about 400 miles away and would take around seven hours.

"I was busy recording this, and thought it would be interesting to show people back here in Aber Tidy.

"We chatted for a few minutes, and then I joined the rest of the guys at a bar. I think you've seen a photograph of us there.

`"Anyway, as we were sinking a few beers, a friendly copper came round the corner and asked us why we were there, where we'd come from in the UK, and all that stuff, and then we asked him if he knew Carlos Botti.

"He went blank. He had no idea who we were talking about. So we gave him a graphic description, but even that didn't help.

"It was only when I showed him what I had just recorded, and pointed to Botti, that his face suddenly lit up, and he shocked us. I recorded it all. Listen to this…"

"'No! No! He not Botti. He Bonetti… Son of Mafia boss Mario Bonetti. Lots [of] money. He not want you to know he's Mafia…

"Family has big, big house in Decumani; in old town. He not live in Milan… He always live here.

"Two brothers. Luca and Giovanni. Luca live in UK, and Giovanni in Spain where family bank the money, and Giovanni in charge.

"Giovanni is known to us. He lives alone in luxury place. Has Ferrari and Maserati, and new powerboat. Now you know all about Mr. Carlos, he won't like that!"

"We thanked the friendly copper, and he plodded up the hill, happily chatting to everyone he saw."

Matthews couldn't contain himself. Botti, a Mafia man, was too much to take. He was visibly shaken, and Griffiths handed him a glass of water

"So, that was his damn motive," said Matthews.

Zach looked at his watch, and gasped, "Wow, it's gone six. I must be on my way."

High fives and lots of back slapping followed before Zach appropriately closed the investigation.

"Must tell you," he said, looking straight at Supt. Matthews, "the killer's signature, Oliva, was not that place in Spain you talked about… Think of it as an anagram."

"Well, well," said Matthews, "it's 'viola'. Now, why couldn't I work that out? Or you, Griffiths?"

Before Zach finally hurried away, he joked, "If BBC Wales come along and want to film this story, Tom Cruise to play me, okay?

" I'd coach a South Wales accent…"

"Brilliant idea," chuckled Supt. Matthews. "And thanks a million for all you've done. And remember the £20,000 reward!"

Aber Tidy slept well that night. Not a single bedroom light burned after 12 o'clock.

And the cleaver was safely back on the butcher's hook…

END

www.ingramcontent.com/pod-product-compliance
Ingram Content Group UK Ltd.
Pitfield, Milton Keynes, MK11 3LW, UK
UKHW042001190726
13854UKWH00005B/2098

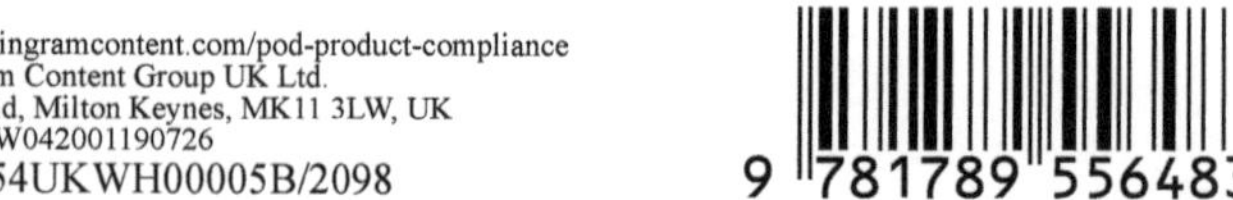

9 781789 556483